S amurai Jack gazed out at the deep blue ocean water. White seabirds dipped above the rolling waves. The bright orange sun hung in the sky just above the horizon.

It was a good day to begin an ocean voyage. Someone else might have taken it as a sign that the voyage would be successful. But Jack knew that there was only one thing he could count on — and that was that he could not count on anything in this strange world.

Suddenly, a loud cry interrupted his thoughts.

"Your voyage is doomed!" an old woman yelled. "No one has ever sailed to the Impossible Islands and lived to return!"

The words sent a chill down Samurai Jack's back. He turned and studied the old woman. A long, black scarf covered her head and shoulders. Her wrinkled face peered out from underneath the scarf.

The woman was addressing a group of sailors on the dock. Some of the men began to whisper to one another in worried tones. But the ship's captain, a tall, wide man with a bushy red beard, just laughed.

"Superstitious nonsense!" he bellowed. "It's that kind of thinking that's kept men out of these waters for the last ten years. Well, the *Mettle* is about to prove everyone wrong. I'd stake my bones on it. Now let's get on board, mates!"

The sailors rallied with a loud cheer and ran toward the ship. The captain started to follow, but stopped when he saw Jack.

"Ahoy, it's our strange passenger!" he cried out. "This old crone hasn't changed your mind now, has she?"

"No," Jack said. "I will go with you."

"Then climb aboard," the captain said. "We'll be sailing soon."

Jack nodded and began to follow the captain. But the old woman ran up and grabbed his arm.

"Beware the Ziphius!" she hissed. Then she darted off and disappeared into the crowd on the dock.

Jack hesitated, but only for a second. He had lived in Aku's world long enough to know that the old woman was probably not crazy. It was likely that real danger waited for him on this journey. But it was a journey he had to take. He climbed on board.

The first few days of the voyage were peaceful. Jack passed the time meditating, sharing the sailors' rations,

and training with his sword. And, as always, Jack imagined the day he would defeat Aku once and for all.

Jack had first encountered Aku long ago, in the distant past, when the evil demon had destroyed his homeland. After years of samurai training, Jack fought Aku and nearly defeated him. But Aku used magic to send Jack far into the future — a future ruled by Aku. The world was now a bleak and dangerous place populated by monsters, mutants, and Aku's fierce robot army.

Jack had to find a way to go back in time so he could defeat Aku and make sure this future never came to pass. That's what had brought him to the *Mettle*. He had recently taken sanctuary with a group of monks who had told him about Tiempo Island. One of three islands known as the Impossible Islands, Tiempo Island was supposed to be home to great hordes of treasure. But that's not what interested Jack. The monks also knew of a special cave on Tiempo Island. Anyone who entered the cave would be able to travel back in time.

It wasn't much to go on, but it was all Jack had right

now. The monks had told him that finding passage on a ship to Tiempo Island wouldn't be easy. The three islands were called the Impossible Islands for a reason. Most ships that sailed there had met with disaster. Fear had kept sailing vessels away for at least ten years.

Luckily for Jack, Pete Redbeard didn't scare easily. The captain of the *Mettle* had put together a crew headed for Tiempo Island in search of the treasure. He was happy to have Jack aboard, although he was suspicious at first.

"You'd best not have any plans on taking all the treasure for yourself," Redbeard had growled.

"I seek no treasure," Jack had said, and Redbeard knew a serious man when he met one.

"Fine, then," Redbeard had said, hand over Jack's. "It might be handy to have a warrior on board. Promise that you'll use your sword to defend us, and you can come along."

Jack had promised, and now he was less than two days from Tiempo Island — and a way back home. That knowledge, along with the fresh salt air and the cheerful sailors, had put his mind at ease for the first time in a long while. Jack took a deep breath and leaned over the ship's rail, watching the boat push through the waves.

"Ahoy, captain!" The cry of the ship's lookout rang through the air. "It's the Impossible Islands!"

Jack looked to the horizon. The lookout was right. A faint sliver of land could be seen in the distance. It must be Minusha Island, the first of the three Impossible Islands, Jack guessed. They were getting closer.

As the sailors cheered, Jack looked back down at the rippling water.

And he froze. Something was not right. The water was bubbling like stew in a pot. Tendrils of steam rose up from the ocean's surface.

Jack ran down the deck to find Captain Redbeard. Suddenly, the bow of the ship reared up out of the water. The movement sent Jack sliding backward. He slammed into the railing, hitting his head on the hard wood.

The blow blurred Jack's vision. He gripped the rail as the ship lurched underneath him once again. All around him, he could hear the screams of sailors.

Slowly, the world came into focus again. A huge monster had risen from beneath the water and now towered over the ship. Fire and smoke poured from its nostrils. Sharp, spiked teeth filled its huge, gaping mouth.

Beware the Ziphius, the old woman had said. Something told Jack that the Ziphius had arrived.

The creature's two armlike flippers swatted at Redbeard and the sailors, who were attacking it with pointed spears. But the weapons bounced off the creature as though it were made of rubber.

Jack rose to his feet. He had promised to use his sword to defend the ship, and now it looked like his sword might be the only weapon that could save them.

Jack ran into the throng of fighting sailors. He drew his sword just as the monster charged into the ship again. This time, Jack kept his balance.

And then he jumped. Jack balanced himself on the ship's rail and swung his sword at the monster's flipper as it moved to swat the ship again. As the sword made contact, Jack heard a familiar metallic sound that told him this monster was not flesh and blood, but a robot.

The Ziphius roared as the sword sliced into it. It

swung back its flipper, and Jack, still clutching his sword, went flying off the boat.

The monster, not used to being attacked, focused all of its attention on Jack. As it turned away from the ship, its massive body caused a huge wave to rise up behind it. Jack watched as the wave carried the ship away.

It was just Jack and the Ziphius now. He raised his sword again and aimed a blow between the monster's eyes.

A hideous scream filled the air. The Ziphius thrashed in the water in a frenzy of anger.

Jack tried to hang on, but the slimy skin of the creature made it nearly impossible. Still clinging to his sword, he began to slide into the churning water. One of the monster's flippers slammed into Jack's head.

And then everything went black.

The first thing Jack realized when he woke up was that he was alive — and dry. He felt soft, hot sand against his skin. He must have washed ashore somehow, probably on Minusha Island.

The next thing Jack realized was that he could not move.

Slowly, his situation came into focus. He was flat on his back. Thin ropes were tied tightly around his body, digging into his flesh. Jack strained his muscles, trying to see if there was any give to his binds.

Nothing. The ropes were thin, but they were tied

tightly and crisscrossed his body like a cocoon. Whoever had tied him up knew what they were doing. The ropes bound all of his muscles securely. The rope was even wound around his fingers, making it almost impossible to flex them.

At least he wasn't tied to the ground. Jack lifted his head as high as he could, scanning his surroundings. Where were the men who had captured him? Then again, they might not even be men. In Aku's world, they could be mutants, monsters, aliens — or worse.

Oddly, there was no sign of life as far as he could tell. He saw plenty of palm trees, but no buildings.

That was just fine with Jack. He was alive, and he was alone, which meant he had time to figure out a way to escape.

Jack studied the situation. Thanks to his extensive samurai training, he knew he could jump from his back onto his feet. But he'd still have to deal with the ropes.

Jack pushed the tips of his fingers into the sand. Where there was sand, there were usually seashells or rocks. Just one sharp stone would do the trick.

Then he felt it. A sturdy clamshell with a broken, jagged edge. Jack picked it up with the tips of his fingers on his left hand and began to saw at the ropes on his side.

Before Jack could cut all the way through the first rope, he heard an unusual noise. A sound like a group of chattering birds was coming from the trees, and it was getting closer.

Jack stopped sawing at the ropes and hid the shell under his fingers. Whoever — or whatever — had captured him might be returning. He didn't want them to know that he was working on an es-cape.

The noise grew closer. It sounded like a lan-guage, but one that Jack had never heard before. Jack raised his head as high as he could, but he could not see anything.

As he lowered his head, Jack noticed something. A small army of what looked like bugs was marching toward him. They were the source of the noise.

As they got closer, Jack realized they weren't bugs at all.

They were people.

Each tiny person was about three inches high. They looked like normal human men, except for their size. Their skin was bronzed by the sun. They wore knee-length pants and brightly colored shirts. Each one held a long, pointed spear in his hand. To Jack, the weapons looked like sharp needles.

One of the tiny men stepped forward from the crowd. He yelled at Jack in the strange language.

"I will not hurt you," Jack said. "Please let me go."

At the sound of Jack's voice, the tiny army let out a war whoop. Their leader shouted something, and Jack felt a sharp pain in his leg as the soldiers poked him with their spears.

Jack knew it was time to make a move. He didn't know how dangerous these Minushans were, but he could tell they weren't friendly.

The samurai used the muscles on his back to propel his body up off the sand. He landed on his feet.

The tiny men poked his ankles with their spears. It stung, but Jack could take it, as long as they could not reach his eyes or face. He used the broken shell in his hand to saw quickly away at the ropes.

As Jack worked, the Minushans used the ropes to climb up his body. He tried to shake them off, but the ropes still bound him too tightly.

Jack sawed. The men climbed higher and higher. Soon he felt one on his shoulder. From the corner of his eye, he saw the Minushan take aim with the spear . . .

And then his left arm was free! Jack swatted the man off his shoulder. The tiny soldier tumbled into the soft sand below. With his free arm, Jack was able to tear off the rest of the ropes in seconds. He shook off the remaining Minushans and then broke into a run.

Incredibly, Jack heard the Minushans' war cry right behind him. Turning, he saw that ten of the soldiers were riding a small, furry pink animal. As the animal zoomed toward Jack, the soldiers held their bows at their sides and sent their arrows flying.

Two of the arrows made contact with Jack's back. He felt a surprising burning sensation on his skin. Still running, he pulled out an arrow and sniffed it.

The arrowheads had been dipped in poison. Jack guessed that such a small amount would not do much damage — but if enough arrows made contact . . .

He picked up speed. Ahead lay the beach and then the ocean. It was his only option. He was a strong swimmer. With luck, he could make it to the next island.

Another arrow struck Jack's leg as he raced into the

water. He dove in and began to swim.

To Jack's dismay, the furry creature knew how to swim, too. There was nowhere to go. Jack would have to stay and fight. But the thought of battling such tiny enemies did not feel right to Jack — even if they did use poison arrows.

"We will help you! Over here!"

Jack turned at the sound of a familiar language. A long, flat boat bobbed on the waves behind him. Piloting the boat was a group of odd-looking creatures. Each one was about three feet high and had a large, flat-topped head. Their legs and arms were small but sturdy. They all had large mouths and eyes, and their features looked as though they were

carved out of dark wood.

"Quick! Get in the boat!" one of them cried out.

Jack only hesitated for a second. The creatures on the boat looked strange, but at least they weren't sticking him with arrows or spears. He swam to the boat and climbed inside.

"Welcome, stranger," said the creature. "We are the Konas."

"I am Jack," Jack replied. "Thank you for helping me."

Jack counted six Konas in the boat. Three sat in a row on the left side, and three sat in a row on the right. They each held a paddle.

"Sit down, dude," said a Kona in the back of the boat. "We need to move before those little dudes catch up. Those furries they ride are good swimmers."

Jack moved to the back of the boat and sat down. The Konas expertly steered the boat away from Minusha Island.

The Kona who had told Jack to sit down turned around to face him.

"I'm Mai," he said. He nodded to the Kona opposite him. "That's my brother Tai."

Jack nodded. These two Konas looked alike. Their heads were shaped like large cubes. Their short bodies were muscular, but Jack still wondered how they managed to hold up their heads at all.

"So, Jack," Mai said, "how did you end up on Minusha Island? We almost never see any biggies there."

"Biggies?" Jack asked.

"Humans," Tai explained. "At least that's the word Layla uses."

Tai looked like he had more to say, but Mai interrupted him.

"So, Jack," Mai continued, "what's your story?"

"I was on board a ship heading for Tiempo Island," Jack said. "We were attacked by a monster."

"Wow!" Mai said quickly. "What did you do?"

"I fought it," Jack said. "But I did not destroy it."

"What about that ship you were on?" Mai asked.

Jack sighed. This little one was full of questions. "I do

not know," he said. "We were separated when I fought the monster. I was knocked unconscious and woke up on Minusha Island."

"We have not seen a ship around here in years," Tai said. "Can you tell us —"

"What's so great about Tiempo Island anyway?" Mai interrupted. "The only thing on that place is a bunch of goats and some shiny rocks."

Jack told the Konas of his quest to find the cave and of his battles with Aku. The islanders listened, captivated, as they rowed toward Kona Island.

Soon the island came into view. Ever since Jack had traveled to the bleak future ruled by Aku, he had not seen much beauty. But Kona Island looked like a paradise.

A sandy white shore rimmed a landscape dotted with tropical trees. As they came closer to shore, Jack could smell the sweet scent of flowers. Their bright colors shone like jewels against the green leaves. Birds and butterflies darted among the blooms.

The boat slid up onto the sand, and other Konas

emerged from the trees to greet their arrival. They began to talk excitedly when they saw Jack.

Mai and Tai hopped out of the boat with the others and dragged it ashore.

"You'll never believe where we found this dude," Mai called out to the others. "Minusha Island!"

The Konas erupted into questions and cries of disbelief. Then a tall Kona stepped out from the crowd. The top and sides of his head were adorned with carvings that looked like long braids.

"I am Kava, King of the Konas," he said. "Welcome to our island."

"I am in your debt," Jack said.

Kava looked Jack up and down, then burst into a laugh that sounded like rumbling thunder.

"We will see, Jack," he said. Then he turned to the Konas.

"We must hold a council meeting in my hut immediately," he said. "Mai, Tai, take Jack to see Layla. Make sure he is treated well."

"Yes, Your Greatness," Tai said.

"Sure thing, Chief!" Mai replied.

Kava and several of the Konas disappeared into the trees. Mai and Tai led Jack down a path in the opposite direction.

"Layla's got her own place," Mai explained. "On account of her being different and all."

Looking at the strange Konas, Jack wondered how different Layla could be. A three-headed monster? A hag with snakes for hair? Perhaps the Konas were leading him into some kind of trap. He put his hand on his sword, ready for whatever lay ahead.

Soon they came to a tall tree with a thick, wide trunk. A tree house made of bamboo reeds and palm leaves sat in the branches.

"Hey, Layla!" Mai called up. "Look what we found!"

A head appeared at the tree house window. To Jack's surprise, it was human.

Layla looked annoyed at being interrupted by Mai, but she froze when she saw Jack.

"Wow," she said finally. Then she threw down a rope ladder that reached the bottom of the tree. "Come on up."

Jack followed Mai and Tai up the rope and climbed through the window. Jack quickly scanned the surroundings. A hammock. Garlands of flowers on the wall. Two bamboo chairs. A small table. And in the center of the table, a photograph of a man, a woman, and a little girl.

The place looked normal, and so did Layla. Long dark hair hung to her waist. She wore a sarong decorated with a flower pattern. Like the Minushans, her skin was bronzed by the sun.

"I haven't seen another human in ten years," Layla said, her eyes focused on Jack.

"We rescued Jack just like we rescued you, Layla," Mai said.

"I was in a shipwreck," Layla explained. "When I was just ten years old. I floated on a piece of wreckage for two days before the Konas found me."

"Jack was in a shipwreck, too," Mai said. "You won't believe his story. You see —"

Layla turned to Mai and Tai. "I'm sorry. Would you two mind leaving us alone for awhile? I have a lot I want to ask Jack."

Mai and Tai shrugged and then headed back down the ladder. Layla sank into the hammock.

"They are like my brothers," she said. "But Mai talks enough to fill the ocean with his words. I would like to hear another voice for a change."

"I understand," Jack said, and once again he told the tale of how he had landed on the shores of Minusha Island.

"That's amazing," Layla said when he was finished. "You're a real-life warrior. I can't believe you have battled Aku." She sighed. "That is one thing I don't miss about my old home. There, we always talked about Aku in hushed whispers. Here, no one speaks of him. It is as though his evil has not touched this place."

Jack gazed out the window at the beautiful trees and flowers. He could almost believe Layla's words were true. Kona felt like some kind of dream.

But a samurai did not have time for dreams. Jack quickly remembered his purpose.

"I must talk to your king," Jack said. "I need to get to Tiempo Island. It is my only hope."

Suddenly, Mai's head popped into the window. Apparently, he had been outside waiting for the two humans all along.

"Sorry, dude," Mai said. "You're not leaving the island. Chief's orders."

"I do not understand," Jack said.

"Don't sweat it, dude," Mai said. "Full moon's coming. Chief says the water's too rough to risk taking a boat to Tiempo Island now. We'll take you there in a few days."

Jack nodded. Inside, he felt the familiar pangs of frustration. He was so close to his goal — yet so far from it.

Layla smiled sympathetically. "It's not so bad, Jack," she said. "You'll be going home in a couple of days. I've been stuck here for ten years."

"Hey!" Mai said. "I thought you liked it here."

"I do," Layla said, patting Mai's head. "Now let's give Jack a tour. If he is going to be stuck here, he may as well have some fun."

As Jack walked among the palm trees with Layla and Mai, he began to relax. His teachers had taught him to pay attention to the natural flow of things. And right now, the flow was slow and easy.

Except for Mai, that is. The young Kona chattered on and on as they walked.

"You picked the right time to be rescued by us," Mai was saying. They sat in the shade, watching a flock of parrots. "The Feast of Pali is two days from now. It happens once every eleven years. I was only a minnow when they held the last one, so I wasn't allowed to go. But I can't wait for this one!"

"What exactly happens there, Mai?" Layla asked him. "I didn't arrive on the island until a year after the last feast."

"It's like a big secret," Mai said. "But if it's a feast, it's got to be fun, right?"

Layla smiled. "I guess we'll find out," she said. "Speaking of feasts, we should get Jack some food."

Jack followed Layla and Mai to the Kona common room, a long, low hut. Jack and Layla had to duck to get inside. But it was worth it. The Konas were eating a delicious feast of fresh fish served with fruit sauces.

After dinner, Layla headed back to her tree house, and Mai and Tai helped Jack find a place to sleep. The Kona huts were too small for him, but Jack was content to sleep on the beach. The two Kona brothers spread soft palm leaves on the sand.

"Dude, you should come with us in the morning," Mai said. "We're going wave riding."

Jack raised an eyebrow.

"You'll like it," Mai said. "We'll teach you how."

"Of course," Tai said.

Then the two brothers disappeared into the night.

Jack stared at the ocean, trying to quiet his mind. It seemed to be filled with questions. Had the *Mettle* survived the attack of the Ziphius? And why wouldn't the Kona chief take him to Tiempo Island right away? He had not seen the chief since he first landed on the island. Something did not feel right.

But the soothing ocean waves did their job, and Jack felt himself growing sleepy. He sank into the sand.

Jack woke hours later to see Mai's face looking into his.

"Wake up, Jack!" Mai said. "The waves are sweet!"

Jack sat up. The sun was just beginning to rise over the horizon. A few of the other young Konas were standing on the beach, looking at the waves. Jack noticed that each one had a wooden whistle hanging around his neck.

Then Layla appeared. She wore a whistle around her neck, too. She smiled when she saw Jack.

"So Mai's got you wave riding?" she said.

"You're going to have to lose that robe, dude," Mai said. "And that sword, too."

"We will see," Jack said.

"Maybe Jack should watch us for awhile," Layla suggested.

Mai shrugged. "Fine with me. Let's just get moving!"

Mai and Tai ran to the water's edge and joined the other Konas. Layla stood with them. They all made a line along the sand.

A shrill sound filled the air as the Konas and Layla blew their whistles. Jack watched, curious.

Suddenly, bright colors became visible on the waves. The colors came closer to shore, and Jack realized they were fish.

They were like no fish Jack had ever seen. Each one was about as long as Jack was tall. But they were flat — maybe three inches thick, Jack guessed, and their backs were perfectly smooth. Each had a rounded head and a flat tail. Some were bright blue, others bright yellow, and some were as green as a palm leaf.

Layla and the Konas waded out into the water. Mai moved the swiftest. He reached out and grabbed a blue fish. He lay on his belly on top of the fish and began to paddle out into the waves with his arms and legs.

The others did the same. Thanks to her longer arms and legs, Layla moved ahead of the crowd.

Several small waves crashed onto the shore, and the wave riders paddled along with them. After each small wave crashed, they paddled out a little farther.

Then Jack noticed a large wave forming in the distance. What could the riders be planning? Surely the wave would swallow them up. He took off his long robe and sword, ready to dive in if he had to.

But the riders did not look nervous at all. In fact, they looked happy. As the big wave got closer, they turned their fish around and began to paddle back toward the shore. As the wave crested underneath them, they stood up on the fish, keeping perfect balance.

Jack watched, amazed, as the wave riders rode on top of the waves toward the shore. He focused on Layla. She stood sideways on the fish, with her knees bent and her arms held out at waist level. Her dark hair whipped in the wind behind her. Jack noticed that she leaned backward and forward to get the fish to move along with the wave.

Next to her, Mai had a huge grin on his face.

"Kona Kona!" Mai cried as the wave broke underneath him. Mai and his fish glided smoothly into the shallow water. Mai tumbled off the fish, and a small rolling wave flipped the fish on its back. Jack saw that the fish had three fins underneath its tail, arranged in a triangle shape. He guessed they helped the fish balance on top of the waves.

"What do you think, Jack?" Layla asked, breathless. "Want to give it a try?"

Jack did not hesitate. In his years of training, he had learned to leap over gorges with the ease of a gazelle; he could run as fast as a cheetah and jump as high as a cricket. It seemed to him that riding ocean waves was something every samurai should know.

Mai whistled again, and a pink fish swam up next to his ankles.

"We'll start here, in the shallow water," Mai said. "Then we'll give it a try with some of the big guys."

Layla stayed back to help. They showed Jack how to climb onto a fish, which Jack learned were called bonzer fish. Mai demonstrated how to jump quickly into a standing position in time to catch a swelling wave. Layla showed the best way to keep balance on a bonzer fish.

Jack practiced all morning. Jumping up and balancing came easy to him. The trickiest thing was sliding onto the bonzer fish, who darted away every time Jack approached.

"She can tell you're a beginner," Mai said. "Don't worry, though. She'll get used to you."

Finally, Jack was ready to try his first wave. He walked out into the water with Mai and Layla, keeping one arm steady on his bonzer fish. They paddled out beyond the smaller breaking waves. Two or three smooth waves rolled in, but none was quite right. Then Mai cried out, "Here comes a sweet one!"

This was it. Jack turned his fish toward the shore and laid down on top of it. He began to paddle swiftly.

"Try to get the bonzer moving as fast as the wave!" Layla called out.

Jack picked up speed, then looked over his shoulder. The wave was getting closer . . .

Finally, Jack felt the wave pick up the tail of the fish. He paddled two more strokes, making sure to keep the head of the fish out of the water.

Jack closed his eyes. Layla had said that timing was everything. If he stood up too early, he would miss the wave. He had to wait for just the right moment . . .

. . . and then it came. Jack jumped up on the fish, making sure to stand sideways as Layla and Mai had taught him. A feeling of exhilaration raced through his body as he rode the wave. Sprays of white foam showered his skin as he skidded to the shore. Jack jumped off the fish into the shallow water.

"Way to go, dude!" Mai called out. He was already paddling back out. "I'm going to catch a few more waves while they're still sweet."

Layla walked up to Jack and smiled.

"Not bad, right?" she said. "I guess I could have picked a worse place to get shipwrecked."

Layla gazed out across the waves. A look of sadness crossed her face.

"I'm not even sure what happened to my family," she said. "I guess I'll never find out."

"It is possible that the *Mettle* made a safe voyage to Tiempo Island," Jack said. "If that is true, they can take you back to your home."

"Thanks, Jack," Layla said. "But this is my home now. I don't know any place else."

Layla did not sound convincing to Jack. He wanted to ask her more, but a loud cry stopped him.

"Help! Shark!"

Layla grabbed Jack's arm.

"Come on!" she said, dashing into the waves. "That's Mai!"

5

Jack scanned the water. Mai's blue bonzer fish was nowhere in sight. Then Jack saw Mai's head bobbing up and down in the waves. A triangle-shaped fin circled Mai, cutting swiftly through the water.

Jack rushed back to the beach and grabbed his sword. Then he plunged into the ocean, quickly catching up to Layla.

"I will take care of the shark," Jack said. "Get Mai to safety."

Layla nodded and held back as Jack swam toward the circling fin. Mai paddled in the water, keeping his eyes on the shark.

"Nice shark," Mai was saying. "Why don't you head out and catch a wave, dude?"

Jack dove under a wave and opened his eyes. The salt water stung, but he couldn't worry about it. He had to find that shark.

And then the gray snout came into view. An image of the shark's sharp white teeth flashed in Jack's mind. This was no bonzer fish.

Jack waved his hand, trying to get the shark's attention. It worked. The creature broke away from its circle and swam toward Jack.

Jack swam backward slowly, keeping his eyes on the shark. He had to draw it away from Mai so Layla could bring him back to shore.

The shark followed, curious, and then its instincts kicked in. It zoomed toward Jack, its huge jaws ready to clamp down on Jack's arm.

Jack was ready. He pushed his sword through the water, and the shark chomped down on the hard metal instead. Any other sword would have shattered from the

assault, but Jack's sword was like no other. It was his father's sword, and it held the power to defeat Aku. One shark was no match for it.

Holding on to the shark, Jack swam up to the water's surface. Gasping for air, he used all his strength to pull the shark out of the water with him.

Watching from the beach, the Konas gasped. From the corner of his eye Jack saw that Mai and Layla were safely on shore. Now all he had to do was get his sword back.

The shark's powerful body thrashed in the air next to Jack. Jack used all his strength to keep his grip on the sword. He just had to get the shark to open its mouth.

Wham! One swift karate chop between the shark's eyes did the trick. The shark opened its mouth, startled. Then it sank into the water, stunned.

Jack knew he only had seconds to swim away before the shark came to. He swam back to shore as quickly as he could, fighting against the pull of the waves. Then he climbed up onto the sand, exhausted.

The Konas let out a triumphant cheer.

"Jack! Jack! Jack!" they chanted.

Mai ran up and beamed at Jack.

"Thanks, dude," he said. "I owe you one."

Jack shook his head. "Now we are even," he said, smiling.

"Wait until King Kava hears about this," Layla said. "He's never going to let you leave our island now. We could use someone like you."

For a brief moment, Jack pictured himself living out his days on the island, spending his time eating fruit and riding the waves. How peaceful that would be.

But outside, in the rest of Aku's world, things were not peaceful at all. Jack still had a job to do. And to succeed, he'd have to get to Tiempo Island soon. Perhaps he could speak to King Kava today.

But there was no chance. The Konas held a celebration for Jack that night, filled with more food than Jack had ever seen in one place. The young Konas beat on small drums and danced. King Kava and his council sat in the shadows, talking. Their mood did not match the happy spirits of the others.

Jack tried to approach them, but a Kona guard stopped him.

"Chief Kava has orders not to be disturbed," he told Jack. "Enjoy the celebration. We are grateful to you for saving Mai."

The guard handed Jack a hollowed-out coconut shell.

"Here," he said. "Have some fruit punch."

Jack nodded and took the punch. Once again, he would have to go with the flow. He sat on the ground next to Layla and watched the Konas dance. Mai's brother Tai approached them.

"Thank you for saving Mai," he said. "We Konas are brothers with all of the ocean creatures, but we have never made peace with the shark."

Jack nodded. He was beginning to feel sleepy.

"Good night, Layla," he said, rising up.

"Good night, Jack."

Jack walked back to his sleeping spot on the beach. He felt so tired. He sank into a deep sleep as soon as he hit his bed of leaves.

Dreams swam through Jack's mind. He dreamed of riding the waves with Layla and Mai. They sailed across the ocean on the backs of bonzer fish. An orange sun shone in a perfect blue sky.

And then a huge wave rose up in front of them, a wave the color of night. Mai and Layla were swallowed up in the blackness as the wave took a familiar shape. Jack opened his mouth, and a scream pierced the air.

Jack woke up with a start. The scream was not his. It was Layla's, he was sure of it. But that was not the only thing wrong.

Jack was no longer in his bed on the beach. He was deep underground, at the bottom of a large hole. In the darkness, Jack could make out a small opening about twenty feet above his head. A circle of woven reeds covered the hole.

He was trapped!

Jack's first thought was not anger. It was sadness. Kona Island was not the paradise it could have been. There was no place safe from Aku's evil.

But that did not matter now. Now he had to escape — and find Layla.

Slivers of moonlight crept through the woven mat above him and cast a pale glow in the hole. As Jack's eyes adjusted, he saw something glimmer on the ground.

His sword. The Konas had not taken it. They must have guessed it would be no use to him here.

But they were wrong. Jack's sword had saved him from many unfortunate situations. He began to form an escape plan.

Jack took off his robe and rolled it into a long, tight rope. He tied one end to the handle of his sword.

Jack looked overhead, took aim at the opening, and sent the sword flying upward.

Perfect! The sword sliced through the opening, leaving the handle and robe-rope dangling underneath. Jack would have to jump — the robe was still about five feet over his head. But he could do it. He just had to hope that the woven mat could hold his weight.

Jack jumped straight up

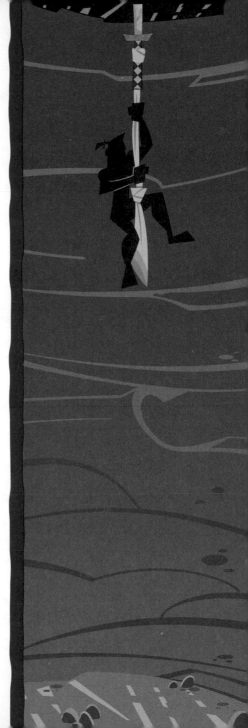

and grabbed onto the end of the robe. Then he climbed. The mat strained, but it held. When Jack reached the top, he pushed the mat aside and climbed out.

Mai and Tai were standing there, frantic and out of breath.

"Jack!" Mai cried. "Something really weird is going on here!"

"I am sure Jack has figured that out on his own," Tai said.

As the brothers talked, Jack quickly freed his sword and put on his robe.

"Where is Layla?" he asked.

"That's what's weird," Mai said. "See, I couldn't sleep. I was too excited about the Feast of Pali tomorrow. So I left my hut and went to find Layla."

Tai shook his head. "Always breaking the rules, Mai."

"It's a good thing I did," Mai continued, talking so fast that Jack could barely keep up. "When I got to

Layla's tree house, I saw six guards dragging her out. She was screaming. I would have fought them myself, but then I thought it might be better to get you.

"So I came to find you, and I saw some more guards taking you here. You were fast asleep," Mai said.

Jack remembered the fruit punch the Kona guard had given him. "I see," he said.

"So then I got Tai. And then we came here. And here we are," Mai finished.

"You still didn't answer his question," Tai said. "Mai saw them bring Layla to the other side of the island."

"Let's go," Jack said.

Mai and Tai led Jack across the island. Things seemed eerily quiet, except for the sound of the two Kona brothers crashing through the island plant life. The full moon shone brightly overhead, lighting their way.

After some time, the trees thinned and Jack felt soft sand under his feet. A new beach stretched out before them. Jagged rocks jutted from the shallow water, forming a kind of wall that reached far into the sea. An orange bonfire burned at the water's edge. Several Konas danced around it.

Jack gently pushed Mai and Tai behind a large rock so they could all take cover.

"Those dudes are members of the council!" Mai said in a harsh whisper. "What are they up to?"

"Maybe they are preparing for the Feast of Pali," Tai said. "I have always wondered why they are always so secretive about it. I think we will find out soon."

"Who cares?" Mai said. "We need to find Layla. Can you see her?"

Jack studied the scene. The leaping flames of the bonfire lit up the beach, but Layla was not in sight.

Then he noticed several small boats moving in the water. His eyes followed the movement of the boats to a large rock several yards from the shore.

Some of the Konas in the boats carried small torches. As Jack watched, the torches circled the rock, bathing it in pale light. The flickering torchlight revealed a figure tied with ropes to a sharp point at the top of the rock. The figure thrashed and screamed.

"Layla!" Mai cried, racing out onto the beach.

Several Kona guards emerged from the darkness. Two tackled Mai, pinning him to the ground. The others ran toward Tai and Jack.

They tackled Tai easily. Jack drew his sword, ready to fight. Then he felt a sharp prick on his leg.

Jack looked down. A Kona guard held a spear to his skin.

"Minusha poison," the guard said. "This spear tip contains a dose strong enough to kill you in seconds."

Jack nodded and lowered his sword.

And then he kicked out. The Kona guard sailed through the air. He landed in the water with a splash. Jack plucked the guards off Mai and Tai, tossing them into the sand.

"Thanks, Jack," Mai said. "Now let's get Layla."

Jack, Mai, and Tai raced down the beach. As they neared the water, the Konas stopped their dance. One Kona stepped forward, blocking their path. It was King Kava.

"Stop!" Kava cried. "No one may disturb the Feast of Pali!"

"This is the Feast of Pali?" Mai asked. "Tying Layla to a rock?"

"Please listen to me," Kava said, looking at Jack pleadingly. "We do not want to hurt Layla. But we have no choice."

"There is always a choice," Jack said. "But some choices are harder than others."

Kava hung his head. "This choice is too hard," he said. "You must understand. Every eleven years, the great beast Pali rises from the ocean. If we feed Pali, it leaves us unharmed. But if we do not feed it, it will destroy us all. We will all die then. What is one life when so many can be saved?"

"Feed Pali?" Mai asked. "What do you feed it?"

Tai nudged Mai with his elbow and motioned toward Layla on the rock. "You can't do this to Layla!" he cried. "She is one of us!" Mai cried angrily.

Kava shook his head. "Pali craves a human feast. In years past, we were always able to find a fisherman or pirate to serve the beast. But since Layla's shipwreck, no other ships have passed by here."

Kava turned to Jack. "Your arrival here caused great confusion. Some of the council wanted to take you to Tiempo Island right away, but others were too afraid of the beast. You would have been our sacrifice, but we thought you would put up too much of a fight."

"You were right," Jack said.

"Is there nothing I can say to stop you?" Kava asked.

"No," Jack said. Then he turned toward the water and jumped inside a boat. Mai and Tai jumped in with him and grabbed the paddles.

"But I will still try," Kava said, "Kona! Kona!"

All of the Konas rallied, and began chasing after Jack. A spear whizzed past his ear. Mai and Tai paddled furiously, sending the boat zipping through the water. Jack fought defensively, deflecting spears with his sword and pushing away any boats that came near.

Finally, they came to the large rock. Jack looked up.

Layla was gone. Only a pile of rope could be seen on top of the rock.

"Layla!" Mai called out.

Layla's head popped out of the water.

"It's about time," she said, climbing into the boat.

Mai and Tai dropped the paddles and hugged Layla.

"You are safe," Tai said.

"But not for long," Layla said. She turned to Jack. "I want to go with you to Tiempo Island. But we've got

to hurry. Kava says Pali will come at the morning's first light."

"Layla, you can't leave us!" Mai pleaded.

"I have to, Mai," Layla said. "I could never feel safe here again. At least on Tiempo Island there is some hope for me."

"What if the *Mettle* is not there?" Jack asked.

"I thought of that," Layla said. "If the ship is not there, I will go back in time with you."

"Layla is correct," Tai said. "She must leave. Tiempo Island is only half a day's journey away."

"Right," Mai said. "And Tai and I are going, too."

Jack started to pick up a paddle, but stopped.

Yes, he was a few hours away from Tiempo Island. A few hours away from the time cave that would take him home.

But if he left now, Kava and the Konas would certainly be destroyed. Perhaps the king did not deserve his help. But should all the Konas suffer for the actions of one?

Jack looked at Layla.

"Go to Tiempo Island," he said. "I will come later."

"Later? Jack, what are you talking about?" Mai asked.

Jack climbed out of the boat and stepped onto the rock.

"I will take Layla's place," Jack said.

" Jack! You can't just let some monster eat you!" Mai exclaimed.

"I do not intend to be eaten," Jack replied.

Layla climbed out of the boat and put a hand on Jack's shoulder.

"Please," she said. "If we go now, we will all be safe."

"But the Konas will not," Jack said.

Layla understood. "Then I will stay, too," she said.

"So will we," Mai said.

"Yes," Tai agreed. "We will."

Jack convinced them to return to shore while he waited for Pali to arrive. He did not want to be distracted by concern for the safety of his friends. Reluctantly, Layla, Mai, and Tai paddled the boat back to shore.

Jack watched as Mai talked excitedly to King Kava, explaining what Jack planned to do. The Konas lined up along the water's edge, staring at Jack with respect and awe. Layla stood several feet away, wearing a look of worry and anger.

Jack climbed to the point on the rock where Layla had been tied. He stared out at the ocean, watching the sputtering torchlight flicker on the gentle waves. The water seemed so peaceful, but Jack knew it was deceiving. Soon a hideous monster would emerge, hungry for his flesh. He did not know what he would be facing or how to defeat it.

Jack gripped his sword and waited. Soon, the first rays of dawn crept over the horizon.

And then suddenly, Jack noticed that the water around him had begun to bubble. Steam rose from it as though it was boiling. Jack gasped as the realization hit him. Could Pali and the Ziphius be one and the same?

The Ziphius answered Jack's silent question with a load roar as it rose out of the water. Jack ducked as the monster shot a hot flame just over his head.

Jack leaped off the rock, swinging his sword as he jumped. But the Ziphius swatted him aside with one of its huge fins, sending Jack splashing into the water.

Jack regained his coordination quickly. He climbed up on a smaller rock as the Ziphius lunged after him. Jack swung his sword again.

Crunch! This time he made contact, ripping a gash in the side of the robot monster. The impact sent Jack tumbling off the rock and into the water again.

Above him, the Ziphius let out a furious wail. Jack guessed it was not used to having its food fight back.

But one blow would not be enough to take down the creature. Jack was faced with a real problem. It was difficult to swim and attack at the same time. And the way the Ziphius moved in water, Jack would need to be able to move after it.

He did not have time to strategize, however. The Ziphius lunged at Jack again, snapping at him with its enormous jaws. Jack dove into the water to escape the attack.

The Ziphius dove after him, fire blasting from its nostrils. Jack shot up to the water's surface and swam swiftly to another rock.

Then Jack saw a flash of pink zipping along the top of the water. It was a bonzer fish — the same one Jack had trained with the day before.

The fish stopped in front of Jack, waiting for him to climb aboard. Jack jumped on the fish's back just as the Ziphius rose out of the water again. A crest of water

swelled underneath them, but Jack was able to keep his balance on the bonzer fish's back. He lifted up his sword and aimed another blow at the Ziphius.

The robot monster blocked the blow with its fin, but Jack still did some damage. Black smoke poured from the injured fin.

"Good one, Jack!"

Layla paddled up next to him on the back of a green

bonzer fish. Mai and Tai rode fish just behind her. They all carried sharp Kona spears.

"We thought the bonzers might be able to help," Mai called out over the roar of the Ziphius.

Jack thought about telling his friends to return to the shore, but realized he didn't have to. Any who were brave enough to get this close to the Ziphius could take care of themselves. Still, he was not sure what they could do.

"Your spears will not harm it," Jack called back.

"That's okay," Mai said. "We'll keep it busy so you can harm it all you want!"

That gave Jack an idea.

"Can you draw the monster to the shore?" he asked.

Mai nodded. "Sure thing!"

By now the Ziphius had forgotten about its injured fin. It lunged at Jack once again. Layla, Mai, and Tai paddled farther out into the water, where the morning's first waves were beginning to swell.

Jack jumped off his bonzer fish, delivering another blow to the monster's belly. His sword pierced the

63

Ziphius there easily, releasing another puff of black smoke. Jack guessed he had found a weak spot.

Perfect, he thought. They might have a chance. Getting the Ziphius into shallow water would give them the advantage they needed.

"Kona! Kona!"

The Ziphius turned away from Jack to see Layla, Mai, and Tai riding a wave toward the shore. It dove into the water after them, disappearing underneath the waves. Jack began swimming toward the shore, too, trying to catch up to his friends.

Suddenly, the Ziphius rose up behind them all. Its giant form blocked out the rising sun.

Jack had reached shallow water. He ran past Layla, Mai, and Tai, his sword raised high above his head.

With his feet planted firmly in the sand, Jack delivered a fierce blow to the monster's belly. The Ziphius wailed, then crashed on its back, drenching Jack, his friends, and the Konas on the shore.

The cold water seemed to snap King Kava and the

Konas awake. They charged into the water, waving their spears. Black smoke filled the air as the Konas used their spears to tear the robot monster to pieces.

"Dude, that Pali beast is weird," Mai said, watching from the beach. "I've never seen a living beast breathe fire or bleed smoke."

"It is not a living beast," Jack said. "It is an evil robot creation. There are many like it in Aku's world."

"Yes," Layla said softly. "Aku's evil poisons every corner of the planet. If it wasn't for that monster, this place might have been a paradise."

King Kava arrived back on the beach in time to hear Layla's words. He hung his head in shame.

"I am sorry, Layla," he said. "Is there anything we can do that would cause you to forgive us?"

"There is one thing," Layla said. She looked at Jack. "We need to get to Tiempo Island!"

Mai and Tai insisted on being the ones to take Jack and Layla to Tiempo Island. It wasn't long before they were under way. Layla had stuffed a pack with a few clothes and the picture of her parents.

"I wish I had a picture of you two," Layla told Mai and Tai as their boat sailed toward the island. "I will miss you both so much."

"Do you have to go, Layla?" Mai asked.

Layla nodded. "I want to look for my family."

"What if you don't find them?" Tai asked.

Layla patted Tai's head. "Now that the monster is gone, I am sure I can find a boat to take me back to Kona

Island. That is, as long as King Kava does not have any more plans for me."

"The young Konas are having a meeting tonight," Tai said. "King Kava and the council have a lot to answer for."

The sun had reached its highest point in the sky when Tiempo Island came into view. Unlike Kona Island, which was flat and sandy, Tiempo Island had a hilly, rocky surface. That was a good sign, Jack thought. Where there were hills and rocks, there were usually caves.

As their boat got closer, they saw another good sign. The *Mettle,* Pete Redbeard's ship, was anchored just off-shore. It looked to be in one piece.

"Is that —" Layla began. She was too excited to speak. Jack nodded.

"I was almost hoping it wouldn't be here," Mai said sadly. "But I'm glad you'll get your wish, Layla."

"Thanks, Mai," Layla said. "I hope Jack gets his wish, too."

A happy sight awaited them when their boat reached the beach. Pete Redbeard and his crew sat around a camp-fire, roasting fish, eating fruit, and singing songs of the sea. Stacked up around them were canvas sacks bulging with sparkling stones.

The men stopped singing when they saw the Konas' boat approach. Then Pete Redbeard stood up.

"By Neptune's boots!" he exclaimed. "If it isn't our brave warrior."

Redbeard slowly walked toward Jack, then poked a finger in his chest.

"You're not a ghost, are you?" he asked.

"No, he's not!" Mai said. "And neither are we."

Redbeard gave Jack a fierce hug, lifting his feet off the ground. Then he released Jack.

"Come say hello to Jack, boys!" Redbeard called back to his crew. "It seems there is no end to our good fortune."

The sailors dragged the travelers back to their fire and made Jack tell them how he had survived the Ziphius. Actually, Mai did most of the explaining, which was just fine with Jack. In turn, Redbeard told Jack that the Ziphius did not pursue them after Jack vanished overboard. The ship had been tossed by strong waves, but they had soon regained control and had reached Tiempo Island safely.

"It's everything we dreamed, Jack," Redbeard said. "Treasure for the taking. You can take a share if you like. It's the least we can do for you."

"No, thank you," Jack said. "But you may do one thing for me. Please see that my friend Layla returns safely with you."

"On my honor," Redbeard promised. "But if you aren't looking for treasure, then what are you looking for?"

"A cave," Layla said. "Have you seen one?"

Redbeard stroked his chin. "Sorry. I can't say that we have."

"I know where the cave is," Mai said.

Tai nodded. "It is true. The bonzer fish have a colony on the far tip of the island. There is a cave just beyond the cove."

"Tai and I can take you there," Mai said. "Then we've got to get back before it gets dark."

Layla knelt down and hugged the brothers. "I will not forget you," she said.

"You can come back to Kona whenever you want," Mai said. "We'll make sure you're safe."

"I know," Layla said tearfully. Then she turned to Jack.

"I will not forget you, either. I hope you get to go home, too."

Redbeard and the sailors cheered as Mai and Tai sailed away with Jack. Mai was unusually quiet as he paddled.

Finally, they reached the cove. The land curved deep into the island. At the far end, Jack could see the dark opening of the cave.

The water in the cove was calm, barely rippling beneath them as they glided over it. Pink and orange bonzer fish floated peacefully on the water's surface. Mai and Tai piloted the boat between the sleeping fish. When they arrived at the end of the cove, Jack climbed out of the boat.

"Thank you," Jack said.

"Too many good-byes today," Mai said sadly. "Take care of yourself, Jack."

"Yes, Jack," Tai said. "The Konas thank you."

Jack watched as the boat glided out of the cove. Mai waved good-bye as the boat disappeared from view.

Jack turned to face the cave. From the outside, it

seemed like an ordinary cave. He stepped closer to the entrance.

Strange carvings were etched into the rock around the opening. Jack detected a faint humming noise coming from deep inside the cave. As Jack peered inside, he saw a pale blue glow within the darkness.

Jack's heart began to beat faster. This had to be the cave he was looking for. Jack took a deep breath and stepped inside.

"Not this time, Samurai Jack!"

Every cell in Jack's body filled with dread at the sound of the voice. He slowly turned around.

A giant black wave towered high above the cove, poised to fall. At the top of the wave grinned a familiar face. Red flames leaped above bulging white eyes. Sharp fangs gleamed in a gaping mouth.

"Aku!" Jack cried.

Aku had the power to take any form. Jack had seen Aku become all kinds of monsters. But something about the giant wave was especially terrifying. Jack knew it could sweep away his dreams in an instant.

"How does it feel, Jack," Aku asked, his voice echoing in the cove, "to be so close, and then lose everything?"

"I have not lost yet," Jack replied.

Holding his sword in front of him, Jack ran and then jumped over the water. Below his feet, he could see the bonzer fish swimming swiftly out of the cove.

"*Aaaaaaaaaaaaah!*" Jack let out a powerful yell as he flew through the air, swinging his sword at Aku.

Before Jack could make contact, Aku evaporated before his eyes. He landed in the cove with a splash. Jack jumped to his feet, startled. Then Aku took the form of a wave again, rising up between Jack and the cave entrance.

"I am not here to destroy you," Aku said. "Only to destroy all hope."

Then the Aku wave swelled even higher. Jack knew he was powerless to stop it. In seconds, the cove — and the cave with it — would be submerged.

Jack's survival instinct kicked in. He swam out of the cove as fast as he could.

A thunderous sound filled his ears as Aku crashed down, enveloping the cove in water. The force of the crash propelled Jack forward, several yards offshore.

I can swim to land, Jack thought, turning toward the beach. *I will go back and find Aku. This is not over.*

But it was. Aku's dark shape blocked the sun as a new black wave rose up from the water. This one was ten times bigger than before. Aku let out an evil laugh as he

towered over Tiempo Island.

"Say good-bye to all hope!" Aku cackled.

The Aku wave began to rise and swell. The demon would destroy Tiempo Island just to spite him.

Then a panic rose in Jack's chest. There was no way he could survive such a wave. Nor could his friends.

"Jack! Over here!"

The *Mettle* had set sail. Layla and Pete Redbeard were calling his name. Redbeard threw down a long rope.

"Climb aboard, Jack!" Redbeard called out.

Jack swam to the rope and climbed into the ship.

"How fast can we go?" he asked the captain.

"The wind's in our sails, mate," Redbeard replied. "We'll have to hope that's good enough."

The sky overhead grew black, as if poisoned with Aku's evil. The wind got stronger as Aku circled the island, forming a huge funnel of water.

Jack watched from the ship as the giant funnel collapsed, sending huge waves rippling out into the sea. They shook the *Mettle,* but the ship held fast.

Then the sky overhead turned from black to blue. The waves grew calm.

The horizon was empty. Tiempo Island was gone.

"I'm so sorry, Jack," Layla said.

Jack said nothing. He lowered his head, overcome with despair.

"You will find a way," Layla said softly. "I know you will."

Jack did not speak for a long time. Then he raised his head.

"I will find a way," he said. "And when I do, Aku will pay."